To order additional copies of this book, contact:
Xlibris
1-888-795-4274
www.Xlibris.com
Orders@Xlibris.com

Features Rideshare stirring by Ed. and Aeron,

Mohammad Shushari

A Kiss to Remember

The beginning feels bizarre to me likewise the end, and I am all over it. After my class or lab, I head to my app, hoping to make some money for a few hours before sticking to my homework. The earlier I receive the request, the less time and gas I waste. Touch Start here. It is ringing! It is Erica. Location is within one of the tech companies. Let's meet with this character. She is approaching the door. She looks pretty—mild dark gold or tan skin with an adorable face.

"Hi, is this for Erica?" she says.

"Yes, I am Ed. Come in," I say. What a lady! And she is sitting next to me. My hair is neat today. I have spent some time on it. Hopefully it pays off.

"What a meeting we had," Erica says. She exhales wine from her mouth. "The new government is trying to remove support from elementary schools." She disagrees with that, and I have no idea about this legislation.

Citizens want to gain more services for all no matter what the government's plans are to cut off expenses here and direct money to another direction. So I shall keep the current educational support. I don't have kids. I mean, I don't care. But I will her with her. Ten minutes passed, and it is a sunny day. Something strange is going on. I am not used to this appeal to chemistry. She ends up cuddling my shoulder. I will let that touch pass as innocent as she appreciates the good conversation we are having.

As we are driving on Highway 405 south, she takes my right hand and starts to chuckle it carefully, taking all parts of my dorsal hand. Honestly, I have not had my hand touched that way before. My hand is being kissed as she searches for those blond hairs. This is magnificent. I have no imagination for happening that at all. I am driving nonetheless and don't want to engage more into this. I steal a look occasionally to this attractive face, trying to decode what ideas are in those pleased eyes. She is coming closer and perhaps aspiring to lean on my shoulder. I can understand that; I hug her to my lower armpit. She does not deny. Why will she? After all, she wants this.

I am having superiority moments. To return the favor, I take her hand and give her a kiss. But it is not in that depth she started with. She owes me one. She is excited.

We are far, about six miles from the drop-off point. She is kissing my shoulder. I really want to blow her that kiss, but I cannot. I wish there is a signal light or terrible traffic so I can slow down. I think I shall be more professional and continue this amazing ride safely. We are listening to Bryan Adams. She wants me to play "Have You Ever Really Loved a Woman?" I have all tracks except this one. But I have got to find it. I must play it. YouTube is easy. Bring it. Here it is. I like all the hits here except "Summer of '69," which is faster and not fit for this romantic scene. This is not the rule of thumb in getting such a lady. I don't know. It is one of life's coincidences. I have no clue.

She is asking me to stop by a gas station just prior to her home to buy some groceries. I need to pull over and stop this fantasy thing before I collide. We are leaving the highway, finally going on minor streets. Here is the place where she picks up her beer and stuff. She is relaxing as we we keep on touching all the way. She is on her back, stretching. It's the best position to kiss. Despite the wine smell, I need to taste those lips for my great memories—a day hero driver's memories! I am approaching gray area, and she is closing her eyes. My windows are not shaded. We lack privacy. It is fine. It's afternoon now. There are no neighbors that identify through the scene. We just kiss. Yes, warm lips. She has melted. With closed eyes, both vulnerable, yes, we are proceeding. We kiss for a few minutes.

"Oh! You just kissed me," she says.

"Oh, really?" I laugh, and that is all that.

Flashback

Switching a job might be a precursor to success. I was flipping burgers never had a good spring until I met a man called Joe, who offers me a new opportunity. Joe does not want to offer this job without getting a bonus of $400 if I complete ninety successful rides in the first month. My eyes pursue this gift too; it will help me a little bit in starting this business for essentials. Or I can put them aside in case my car breaks. He emails *Briskly* with my email information. They email me back to sign up. I upload all the documents they need: car insurance, registration, my info, and a photo. I cannot wait for the next few days in which Joe wants to take me to the hub and continue filing the necessary documents. He rents me his car for a thousand monthly. I shared with him my family plan's insurance and cell phone accounts. Those are the requirements to drive.

My phone sucks. The screen is not glossy, and throughout the day, it is hard to see the routes. I can handle all the troubleshooting together; I just want to start. I think it takes a couple of weeks to get the background check done. I shall sign up for "Good to Go." The toll bridge charges roughly three dollars to pass. With a "Good to Go" sticker, I only have to pay about half. I sign up for too many things. I am excited though. I finally can depolarize into making some extra money.

I share a two-bedroom house with a man who has three kids. The kids make it to our place on weekends. He is divorced, and that's the court's decision on the kids' visiting terms. I play video games with them, babysitting until not far from now. My roommate is a hard worker in the field of electromechanics. I learn some electric stuff from him. At almost 5:00 p.m. daily, we finish. I go upstairs, bounce my knee up, and tickle my body on my bed until forever! I detailed dry cleaning vehicles for a while. Edward became a badass.

I love to ride the bus daily. Half of the passengers in the bus are the same as me—students who leave home for different purposes. If I drive that midsize SUV, I won't ride the bus anymore. I am used to these early morning faces. It is early Tuesday; my will wants to wake up, but my body does not. I cleaned a van last night, twelve hours from toe to toe, earning $120. I need to catch bus 245, or I will have to wait thirty minutes more.

My class starts at 7:45 a.m. Finally, I am outside. It is okay to be a couple of minutes late. I can catch up with Denise. She is my study partner. She has different guy friends for different purposes. Finally, I make it to my class. I am wearing the local team jersey; a public figure seems to be in my classmates' eyes. My body and my voice are still up as I am still running. I answer a couple of questions. Stress brings wishes and makes a day.

"Denise, how about a cup of tea? It is my treat."

"Sure," she says.

She requests tea within double curtain cups to isolate us more, maybe. Clever girl. I have no doubt about her. We chill a little bit. It's time to go home. AJ is changing a timing belt. That is six hours of work at least. He assigns me to work right away. He usually gets stuck in the last bolt in most vehicle brands! It is that tough to play with these ruthless steels during this cold winter. He gets frustrated. Then he gets happy. He fluctuates between both mental states. At the end of a long day, I lie on the bed, a master of myself. I need to go in depth on this material. Some proportion belongs to the homework and some to the actual work, and both, at some point, are irrelevant as a student sails to the unknown. Sometimes I am wrong. Can the instructor be wrong, and there's no harmony between homework and the work? I am waiting for that background check. My instructor tells me not to bike at winter. I believe her. I shall follow her on whatever social media applies. This home is crowded most of the time. AJ is a very social person. He cooks from scratch and invites people. Sometimes, I feel the need to get out of this situation just for the sake of some privacy.

As Halloween is approaching, I am hoping to have a date with Denise. She is hanging out with another person for concerts, movies, and perhaps other things that I don't know. I don't think she is in love. I will not betray a dude. Her eyes are on me; I ought to figure it out. For the dress code, I am into using some fancy ties a couple of times weekly. She is wondering why I am dressed up. I tell her, "During the weekend, I got a job in a town called Dexter and started on Sunday."

I capture a sentence from her eyes—ideal guy who gets the job done in a timely manner. She says, "My parents live in Dexter

"How do you commute to get there?"

She says, "I bought a little car manufactured in 2001. The owner is working in the tech field. He assigned his wife to meet me and relinquished the car title."

She cannot hide that jealousy in her eyes; that unregulated my confidence and wishes. I do not negotiate the contract. I am determined to proceed and learn some stuff related to the medical industry. I put off Uber's application, or Uber ignored mine. Lindsey does not save compliments when seeing me with those silky ties. The instructor listens carefully and tracks Denise's expressions. She is dating one. I get only compliments—not fair game. Next Thursday is an optional class. You are welcome to come in but for a friendly social talk. I am done of waking up at 7:00 a.m. I do not estimate any consequences.

It is Thursday. I decide not to go. I just go to my work. It is Friday. Just before my class, I have a little talk with Lindsey in front of the classroom. Denise comes and doesn't say anything. She enters the classroom. A minute later, I follow Lindsey. I glance at Denise talking with the guy behind me and say, "I want to sit next to you." He looks at me and hesitates. He welcomes her anyway. She leaves her seat. Denise leaves me. She thinks I dated Lindsey since Lindsey was absent on Thursday too! I keep the space between me and Lindsey, keeping Denise's place unfilled until the end of the quarter.

I have to walk miles and miles across that town for many years. Rain is a normal case. Flu is associated with me each fall-winter alternate. I eat pomegranate to protect myself. It works in most cases. Mediterranean food is eaten to cover all seasons around. I miss driving cars; riding a bus or walking is tolerable. I sell my car. I quit a job that offers fourteen days of yearly vacation. You need, furthermore, to apply one year beforehand to earn it. You need to define the time of start and end.

It's fall, and I'm taking chemistry class. I work the first month with Hailey, then she works with a girl. I am working with Jessi, an Asian girl, now. We have a lab. I am observing the temperature of the liquid while Jessi is writing the report. Everything is going all right. Hailey just shows up late. She comes to work with me, which I don't understand. Huh? Switching classmates! All three of us work on the experiment. She wants to come back to working with me. Jessi withdraws on the next lab session. She decides to work with another guy. It's my fault for letting Hailey on the team.

I have to follow up on *Briskly*. At least I will get a car to drive. I need the flexibility of working in rideshare. Joe preserves the agreement between us. It is better to go to the hub and accelerate the papers. My background check is available but needs a renewal. It shall be faster this time. Here is Tuesday morning, and I ought to go with Jo and his kid to the hub. AJ wants to join us for no reason. This is the first time they will use the bus to go downtown. Each one has approximately three cars in front of their doors. We take the express to Jackson Street, then walk a bit. I print a number and wait. Those pictures on the wall are of the most loyal and hardworking drivers. The majority are in their late fifties and are African American heroes. I can't be a hero. I just want to support my education as scholarships are scarce. They shoot a photo of me and sign me in. I pick up the car. Joe asks me, "Are you going to drive?" I say no. I am tired. He is confused. But I have a headache and cannot drive. I just go to "Good to Go" and initiate a passing sticker. AJ asks me to park it far since he reserves the space for his clients.

The First Ride

I do not have much idea on how to handle these options. I hesitate in turning the app on. I hope it's a short ride. I have limited time to make some money since I have to go back home to crack my textbook. I finally decide to hit the button. All that I need to do is just to hit that button! I am looking at the trash cans when it starts ringing. How to accept it? Hit anywhere. I accept.

Samantha is not a welcoming person. I put her luggage in the trunk and move. Going through 148th Avenue, sunshine is nailing on my screen. I could not see the next route to the airport. It takes me through a different route—a longer trip. I hit a button on my steering wheel accidentally, and here, a robotic voice comes on. I say, "Shut up now." I wish it's smarter and can interact with me. Sam smiles finally, not for me but for the technology. Sam says, "I want to get out and request another *Briskly*." I understand. We are lost through a longer route.

"No way. I am taking you there," I say. The trip continues until we arrive safely. She tells me that I need to pay attention to the signs. I need to go home after this terrible start. I feel like it did not go well. Technical support emails me, saying, "What happened? It took a longer time." In the evening, I meet with some of the experts in this domain, and I ask for some tutoring on the app and overall customer service. I ask to check my rate. They check it. She gives me one star. That sucks. I stay professional with her anyway. Joe says, "If she was a different person, she would have given you five."

To learn this business, I realize that I need to give *back-to-back* rides and develop a *second nature*. I turn the app on in the evening, hoping to meet nicer ones. I get a request. Alex is a male Russian truck driver who travels across the nation. He wants to stop by the city and doesn't have a desire to drive. I had some classes with Russian ladies before. They were nice to me. So here we go, a short trip of two miles. He will not give me less than four stars. I drive my car the next day to the students' parking lot. What a feeling! It is a 2014 midsize all-wheel drive. I hate the suspension. I can feel any cranky road. The sound system is not giving me the clarity I am looking for. It is time to shut my mouth. I don't have to commute anymore. Occasionally, I approach the middle of the road. The thing is, something is driving me to the opposite direction, and to keep moving forward, I need a force to coupling with my direction driving this truck only to the right, similar to Le Chatelier's principle in chemistry.[1]

It is Saturday night. I turn the app on and get a ride downtown. I say I don't want to get into any risk; therefore, I shall drive back to a smaller, less dense city. On the freeway, I get a request from Renton—folks around the age of seventeen. They appreciate the distance I cross to pick them up. They are partying inside the car. It's all fun. They are heading to Brad Street. I really don't want this trip to end. They introduce me to a different perspective in this domain. Almost at the end, vapor condenses on all windshield directions. Oh, the defrost system is not functioning. I turn the AC on to clear my way. Here we are, Brad Street. She blows me a kiss—five stars for sure. I have a couple of successful rides before heading back home. I cannot stay until the bar closing. I just need to sleep with good memories.

In the lab, while working with Hailey, Hailey says to me, "I want to suck the extra humidity and let the powder dry faster!"

"Okay, go for it."

She says, "Can I suck more?"

I am embarrassed to reply. A student near me glances and smiles. Literally, she is smoking hot. Still, I respect the lab and the lady next to me who is vacuuming too.

Swallowing Salt!

I admit, a one-way direction is confusing in a way that I must back up. I have experienced that a couple of times. You expect a turn, but it's not a turn, and vice versa. I think I will get a complaint. I hope this won't happen again. I do appreciate people who understand and give me another chance. I just give a ride to a guy with a twisted mustache. I am driving fifty miles per hour on the highway. This is a heavy car; thereby, you won't feel speed.

He says, "Speed up, driver."

I glance and see panic in his eyes. I guess he is in pain. I say, "Sure." Anyway, the trip is done. Oh, this is my favorite grocery store. I need some bread and cream cheese. There is a lovely lady who starts a conversation with me. She has a pretty face and white with Garson hair—total package. I enter through the bakery area during the day shift. I am not expecting to see her. She is mostly on night shift, and I'm not sure if it's her off today. I pass through the seafood section and keep going. Here is the Brutus area. I see her again. I thought she quit. I have not been here for a couple of months since I moved. I decide to initiate a conversation this time. I pull a bag of clementine and approach her.

"Is this sweet? Have you tasted it?"

"I have not," she says. I think she is not having a nice day. Then I grab a piece of orange. It looks red, implying a sugary taste. She tells me that this is probably the worst orange that is on sale. She further provides me with a special treatment. She takes it and cuts it, giving me a slice. I taste it.

She says, "What do you think?"

I say, "I give it 80 percent."

She says, "Wow. That is more than what I expected."

She offers me another slice from a different type, and she tastes both. A woman is looking at us, and her eyes fill with bias, which reflects our bias! It's the impartiality of destiny that balances my day. A day can fall between positivity and negativity; if you are having a negative day, stay home or look up for an opportunity. I think that is enough for today, or it is more than I deserve. I tell her, "See ya later, Madison."

She says through bright eyes, "Oh, thank you." I believe that made her day too. All that I need is a table for two. I am into running my car. Yes, I need to work and make some money. I am close to establishing my own place, my love, and my peer. I run the app, but the app is not working. The phone seemingly is having trouble turning on. Not yet. My account is deactivated.

Twenty Years in the Making!

If fun has a stratification, working with Justin earns the highest level. He is a person who does multiple mistakes on a shift. We try to fix things behind him. He types on the screen this: "Grilled cheese, no-bun bowl." I am doing the buns and veggie stuff. I cannot get how to melt the cheese and put it inside an aluminum bowl. I think there is something wrong. I check with him. "Hey, Justin. Are sure this is a no-bun bowl?" He scratches his hair, processing for a while. The customer laughs. I realize that there is something wrong. I leave a comment on the store manager's screen and write on it, "There is something wrong." Heidi knows what kind of fun can pass through the evening shift. Oh man, if you work in a coffee shop and a customer orders mocha and you make Americano instead, then that is it for you. How many times have you gotten fired, bro, if it's not too embarrassing? So this is what we are doing in such a freaking fast-food industry. Through closing time, we enjoy the golden era of the '70s and '80s. I shall stick with this until graduation. I like the neighbors. Most of them are nice. We get customers of postgame teams, both winner and loser, which elevates this atmosphere at work. Working here is such a game—you work on different stations, you get different tasks, you listen to music, you use breaks as needed in a chaotic way!

I have negative reviews on my account. One says, "He was driving forty miles per hour on the highway, which is unsafe." Another says, "He had navigation problems." Therefore, I am suspended permanently. It's easier to complain, harder to praise. I return the car to Joe. Taking organic chemistry with a nice instructor, I can feel days running quickly. He assumes most of the students have part-time jobs. Homework is limited, and most of the work is done during class time. The other class is creative writing, which I elected to fill in requirements. Euphoria—I feel it whenever I finish class then head to my work. In my work, Justin gets lost downtown. He is born and raised up here. It's one of his moments. He comes late anyway after a baseball game. I want to make sure things are right. I tell the manager, "Guess what?"

He says, "What?"

"Justin got lost," I say.

"Where?" the manager asks.

"In your office," I say.

Everybody starts laughing. One hour later, the manager says, "Ed, you know what happened?"

I say, "No, what happened?"

He says, "Justin got lost."

I say, "Where?"

He says, "In the parking lot." This just goes on; we are joking all night. All that I need is more appreciation from Justin.

"Hey, buddy, have you seen the WWE episode when Mr. McMahon told Hulkmania that it has been *twenty years in the making*?"

"Dear, I remember it."

"So I am giving you twenty-years-in-the-making cheeseburger. Go to break."

Nostalgia

Joe wants me back in a new carrier called *Easy Trip*. You have no idea how much I miss driving and meeting new people. All that you need to do is apply online, and they will follow up on you. I submit my application and wait. It takes three weeks to approve my photo! I take the car back and drop it off at the inspection area. It's approved. And why not? It is still 2014. I will click the button and have my first person. I hit it and get a lady from far away—eight miles. She cancels me. I get two more requests that got cancelled. Riders are far from me. *Easy Trip* is a new company and needs more time. I need to grow with them. They are number 2 in the market. I decide to give it my best.

I notice a great connection, and they care about us as drivers. In a great society that seeks satisfaction for all, I am hearing perspective from people who request us because they know that Easy Trip cares about us.

My first ride is to three phony people. I give them more respect than they deserve. They turn me down with four or less stars out of five. I get another ride, and it seems as if they have given me five stars. Easy Trip emails me that I am improving. They care about us.

It is Sunday. The effect of Monday starts in the afternoon. Many do their laundry, personal care, etc. I feel bored; this signal light is not turning green. Oh, it's green now. I shall move, but this bicyclist is not moving. I tap on the horn. She looks at me while carrying food or stuff for delivery probably. She is blond. She looks at me, and she gives me the middle finger. You cannot tap on the horn in this city. You have to stay fixed on the signal light. I maneuver my car and leave. I shall go home before encountering another bad case. I have learned, nonetheless, to count to ten before reacting to any similar situation.

I start the next day with a new strategy. I am feeding my unconsciousness level with only positive statements. Respect pedestrians more, acquire passivity, feed people with happiness in any setting, and so on. I need to delete those negativities and replace them with good ones. Less reaction is equal to minimized harms. This is what we do when we add components in the lab to another—just slowly, no rush. To yearn for the past, the past should be worthy to be remembered.

I am starting Monday early, hoping to give an airport trip and come back safely before my afternoon class. Waking up, I think that starting the engine is not an option in the winter. I shall try the ins and outs of this career. I will not be suspended again. The app is ringing. I will take it. Driving during the dusk gives the advantage of no traffic. Twenty-two minutes later, I am there, dropping off in the airport. Where is the area for waiting and picking up? I am trying to find it, driving around the arrival, departure, and the cell phone areas. I am glancing over fifty-ish Somalian drivers in a spot. I drive there, and it is the waiting area. Should I wait or go? That's the question until a man comes and asks some drivers about this system. They explain to him. He does not like that and says, "Holy crap. I will go back to town." That encourages me to leave. I wait one hour without benefit. I decide to leave. I then generate a rule of forty—if my number in the queue is forty, I wait. If more, I go back to the city.

Orange Image

I really do appreciate people who sit on the front seat. A lady sitting next to me gets many possibilities. She just complains about her coworker who asks her what to wear for a job meeting this evening. She is wondering and asking me why he is asking her. I realize that he is interested in her opinion, but she does not care. She is paying off her undergrad student loan and doesn't want to buy a car and add up a new loan. We are talking as I am driving; a bus is speeding up. She says, "Don't let the bus beat you." At that point, I take it seriously, speeding up and burning the bus driver. She is happy now, but I am not going to ask her if my shirt is neat or not. I am looking at her face and am not noticing any flaw except her nose. But if her nose is one of those royal noses, she will not talk to anybody. Before one mile to end, I say the rest is on me. She shows her appreciation through her sweet talk. It is a stable ride, and I do not want it to end.

I get a request from a group of ladies with one guy. They are in the bar celebrating one of the ladies' birthday. I am playing music, and everybody is cheering. Some start touching me. Somehow, I am involved in this party. I do not notice a Stop sign. I cross it. Woooo! I fail to notice the sidewalk. I jump over it. My car does not disobey. Oh, that is a miss. I shall focus more before I regret anything. They are celebrating her twenty-third, and she asks me for a dance. I accept and but do not know how. I am a little shy; her brother is sitting next to me. She says, "Your hair is ginger." It seems like she likes it. We are close to the end. Before leaving, she blows me a kiss of goodbye.

Riders forgive when it comes to genuine joy. God has protected me after this miss. Hence, no matter how much I am engaged, I promise to pay more attention. I am practicing this now, having folks who are dancing to some of Eminem's hits. I jump the other way. She tells me, "It is okay." Amazing. I am getting forgiveness on such a miss. It's a connection, for certain. I back up my car slowly and move forward. It is after midnight, and this won't happen in the day since the other way will be packed up. My rate is going up, and I am entertaining this city.

Justin Got Fired

I am keeping these three days per week in this restaurant just in case I quench in driving. The manager has asked the owner to raise my wage. I have not taken any promotion since I got hired. I am not that worried about this now as I am advancing in both my work and school simultaneously. Justin is watching a baseball game, which makes him arrive late. He has shared photos on his social media profile related to the game event. Justin denies watching a game. Jose was there with his kids, and he confirms Justin's presence. He gets fired for leaving the team struggling in the line cook at a busy weekend day. I feel locked out without this guy as I am not a Spanish speaker to stay. I am afraid to lose it and lose driving too. At this level, I decide to hang in but limit myself to two days. Training new people is not a very good option. I don't know how managers think in some cases. That guy knows our job. He is highly connected to people and has spent three years in this store. Is it a sensitive job to fire Justin?

Holiday season is remarkable in its momentum. Time is going so quickly. People are moving in different directions, causing a lovely traffic. Lights are displayed everywhere. I wish this is the case all year round. It's so helpful at night. Driving at a foggy night south, I can barely recognize more than a hundred feet ahead. I don't think the color yellow is helpful during a fog. White light is more helpful, to me at least. I wish I can take photos, but I can barely see. The city should make lights adaptable based on the eyes of viewers. It's my bad. I shall not take a far-distance ride. I like short distance. It greatly keeps me regenerated. I finally have arrived. It's 2:00 a.m. now. There is no chance of giving a ride in this city. I am a loser.

I feel loneliness here as I am far. I need to come back regardless of the fog. All good memories are coming while driving north, feeding my subconscious mind. I have many theories in my mind evolving inside this ecosystem. All around me, two mediums are scattered. I am emulsified in two phases. Is that how heaven looks like? God owns time, age, and destinies and can alter them. I am afraid but resist to say. In this cave of a man, I remember closing time with Justin and the rest of the guys. It takes forty-five minutes total time to close the store after serving at least fifty customers, which is enough to secure me in that place. I will get him rehired. I don't want to make an accident as this is Joe's car. I am close to Exit 157. I can see the downtown towers' lights now. I feel safe now; friends are not far to give a hand. This is a journey. This is not a trip.

I don't interrupt people. They are talking about quality moments they had at a bar. A woman sits next to me and starts a conversation about *Jack Reacher*, which intrigues me. "I was not satisfied with Tom Cruise for this role," she says. I am thinking about interrupting now as I am convinced with Tom. Indeed, I watched that movie in the theater.

I say politely, "Why?" I feel that she is trying to synthesize an appropriate answer. I regret that interruption as my rate might go down.

She diplomatically says, "*Jack Reacher* is a story from the *Never Go Back* novel, and the actual protagonist was a massive military sniper.

"Ah, interesting. I have not heard about this novel yet. Sorry about that," I say.

"Of course, he should have been a guy like Hogan or Austin," one of the riders say, "or the Rock. That works too."

To myself, I thought about how I liked an interview of Tom Cruise when he wondered about how the health-care service in Scandinavian countries is advanced.

If it's raining, we'll be busy at this restaurant as usual. If it's windy, we won't be. Social connection invokes customers to come in and see one another through this long winter. We close the store only during a power outage, and we won't be getting paid at that point.

"How come you want me not to deny her dad's tips and her eyes on my eyes during the entire trip? Damn it, Justin. You grew in us that habit of accepting tips. I will not accept tips from her dad. He shows gratefulness in her eyes after all. This is more important to me tonight. I should fill gas, wash my car, and go home."

My Own Car

I am getting tired of this monthly payment and will really buy a car. My mom has an opinion, favoring a new or certified car. I am about to buy some car for about $8,000. It does not have a sunroof. I will listen to my mom. I shall consider a newer car with the most options since I will be staying in it all day.

"It smells great. Not stinky like the instructors' zone," the O-chem instructor says. Students care about their smell more than professors do. Good to know that our professor either is honest or doesn't like his colleagues.

After all, those are the most common questions I get daily:

"So, where you from?"

"Busy day?"

"Do you drive for Briskly or just Easy Trip or both?"

"Which one do you prefer?"

I am dying from people's curiosity, which opens a conversation and has two fatal endings: either we click or thump down, which causes judgment and leads me to be the number 1 stereotyper.

The first stereotype is this: I hate men. They request a ride and track the driver through their phone. "What is this motherf—— doing?" men say. They want to show off their abilities in picking up the right driver. Not to mention, men are better in navigating than women; women are better in designing and organizing, and that might be a stereotype rather than a fact. If I get a request from a man, there is a 50 percent chance that I will get cancelled for different reasons.

For the best stereotype, it comes in reading thoughts. Once, I had a request from hikers on the countryside. A lady sat next to me. Her voice and face were exceptional. I was playing tracks from NSYNC and felt she was melting in this. I am sorry for any sentimentality. I am chatting with myself. I just wanted her to enjoy. The drop-off was the hotel they were staying in. The guy said, "Can we go and bring our luggage, then you can take us to the airport? If you would." I liked this polite request.

I said, "Of course."

I inferred excitement from her eyes. Oh my god, she might sit here one more time, one last time for another sixteen miles. I waited until they came back. I offered gum. They accepted except her. She went through fantasies and daydreams as tracks were played one by one. She was not engaged in her friends' conversation anymore. She shared that she was interested in a double hookup. Her boyfriend called her to assure that she was all right. She said that they were heading to the airport. Two guys were traveling with her for the intramural sport event. Close to the airport, I asked them, "Is it Alaska?"

She was astonished. "You read my thoughts. How did you know?"

I said, "Since you are going to Cali, I expected Alaska as it's common for Northwestern trips."

She said, "Good stereotype."

There Are Many Ways to Go Home—The Best Is a New Way

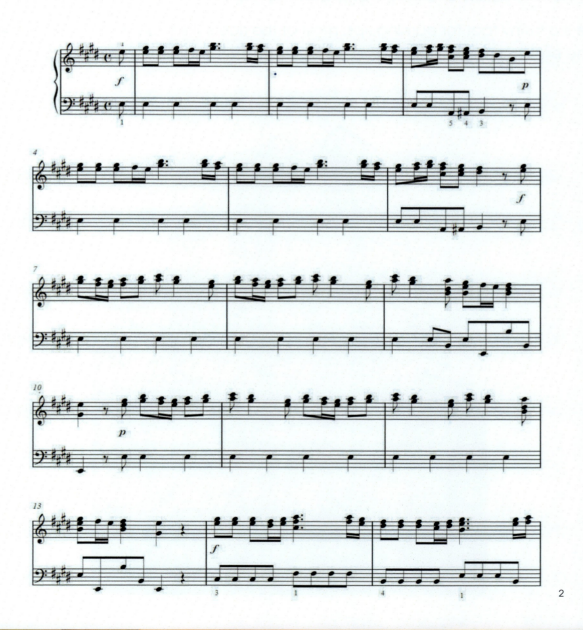

I have not seen a driver like Aeron. He works daily for about fifteen hours. "I start at 3:30 a.m. until 11:00 a.m., then I take a break until 5:00 before going back to catch the night shift," he says.

"Man, why should you do that?" I say. He is middle-aged and has enough money and education. He features a driver whose cars wear off before him. So he updates cars annually. One of his cars got burned! But he was not the driver. He rented that car to a person while he was on vacation. His holistic vehicles remain under service at all times. Like Aeron, I don't respect women on the road. If I give them an opportunity to pass or merge into my lane, they are unthankful. Women, this is the ethical code of driving. We are not establishing love and won't be. Express any form of appreciation. Don't let them pass until they wave, showing respect.

Here's a funny fact for earning tips: most of the riders like Madonna and pay me tips at the end!

That's a Throwback

This city has plenty of one-way directions, and I have a fondness for two-ways. While I am learning this business, I am trying to be happy to please my clients. I release my foot off the gas pedal and hit the Cruise Control button. On this trip, I aim to be in a steady state so that I will receive a new comment or compliment. I want peace of mind on this early day. He thanks me for starting my day early. A family travels, and my playlist is on for things new to me but a throwback for them. It is not a shame to use robotic features. I am still in control and swing this steering wheel left and right. My treat is in the form of bites of chocolates. Kids love that. I like families.

References

Gropper, SS, J. L. Smith, and T. Carr. *Advanced Nutrition and Human Metabolism*, 7th ed. (Boston: Cengage Learning, 2018).

"Success Story: Taxol," accessed on April 3, 2019, https://dtp.cancer.gov/timeline/flash/success_stories/s2_taxol.htm.

Endnotes

1 "Le Chatelier's Principle," accessed on March 30, 2019, https://www.chemguide.co.uk/physical/equilibria/lechatelier.html.

2 "The Four Seasons: Spring," accessed on April 2, 2019, https://www.musicnotes.com/sheetmusic/mtd.asp?ppn=MN0144790.

About the Author

uthor is from Bellevue, WA who finished high school in outstanding Grades, enrolled soon after in pharmacy school, completed prerequisites, from Bellvue College, for the master of the didactic program in Dietetics (DPD), and currently, he is working on his master at Bastyr University in Washington State. He imagines the future of playing a dynamic part of pharmaceutical research, nutrition division to fill gaps in the current researches.

Dr. Mohammad K. Shushari (BSC in pharmacy and pharmaceutical sciences)

Printed in the United States
By Bookmasters